FIX IT, GRANDMA, FIX IT

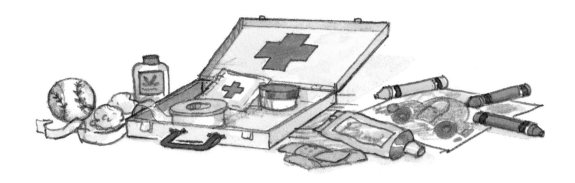

Written by
Kathy Long

Illustrated by
Ann Iosa

Augsburg
MINNEAPOLIS

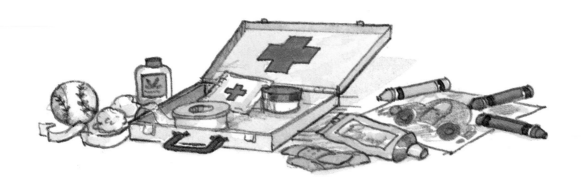

In memory of my own grandma
who could fix anything

"Look, Grandma," Tyrone said.

"I ran too fast."

"Fix it, Grandma. Fix it,"
Tyrone said.

"Bless your heart," Grandma said.
"God will make you feel better."

"I can help Grandpa,"
Tyrone said.

"Grandma can fix it,"
Grandpa said.

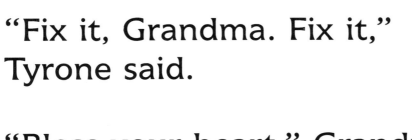

"Fix it, Grandma. Fix it,"
Tyrone said.

"Bless your heart," Grandma said.
"God will make you feel better."

"I have a surprise for you,"
Tyrone said.

"Look, Grandma, I can draw," Tyrone said.

"Fix it, Grandma. Fix it,"
Tyrone said.

"Bless your heart," Grandma said.
"God will make you feel better."

"I can help you," Tyrone said.

"Fix it, Grandma. Fix it,"
Tyrone said.

"Bless your heart," Grandma said.
"God will make you feel better."

"No! No!" Tyrone said.

"Stop it, Max! Stop it!"

"Fix it, Grandma. Fix it,"
Tyrone said.

"Bless your heart," Grandma said.
"God will make you feel better."

"You can fix anything, Grandma," Tyrone said.

"No, I can't, but God can," Grandma said.

"God can help you feel happy when you feel sad.

God can make bad things better," Grandma said.

"God helps you fix things,"
Tyrone said.

"Bless your heart," Grandma said.

"Look, Grandma," Tyrone said.

"Fix it, Grandma, fix it.
And let God help," Tyrone said.

"Bless your heart," Grandma said.
"Bless your heart."

Word List

a	fast	help	sad
and	feel	helps	stop
anything	fix	I	surprise
bad	for	it	things
better	God	let	too
bless	Grandma	look	Tyrone
but	Grandpa	make	when
can	happy	Max	will
can't	have	no	you
draw	heart	ran	your